Lit C

TIGERELLA

D1421369

TIGERELLA

~ KIT WRIGHT ~

PICTURES BY
PETER BAILEY

Hippo

Scholastic Children's Books,
Scholastic Publications Ltd,
7-9 Pratt Street, London NW1 OAE, UK

Scholastic Inc.,
555 Broadway, New York, NY 10012, USA

Scholastic Canada Ltd,
123 Newkirk Road, Richmond Hill,
Ontario, Canada L4C 3G5

Ashton Scholastic Pty Ltd,
PO Box 579, Gosford, New South Wales,
Australia

Ashton Scholastic Ltd,
Private Bag 92801, Penrose, Auckland,
New Zealand

First published in hardback by Scholastic Publications Ltd, 1993
This edition published 1994

Text copyright © Kit Wright, 1993
Illustrations copyright © Peter Bailey, 1993

ISBN 0 590 55670 3

Typeset by Rapid Reprographics
Printed and bound in Hong Kong

10 9 8 7 6 5 4 3 2

All rights reserved

Kit Wright and Peter Bailey have asserted their moral right to be identified as the author
and illustrator of the work respectively, in accordance with the Copyright, Designs and
Patents Act, 1988.

This book is sold subject to the condition that it shall not, by way of
trade or otherwise be lent, resold, hired out, or otherwise circulated
without the publisher's prior consent in any form of binding or cover
other than that in which it is published and without a similar condition,
including this condition, being imposed upon the subsequent purchaser.

ELLA

Ella was nice at the barbecue party,
Everything Ella did
Was right.

She handed round the sausages
And *didn't* give
The dog a fright.

She didn't tease the old tom cat
Or stamp on old Mr Rathbone's hat,
She never, ever did things like that

As *some*
Would have thought
She might.

No,

Ella was *fine* at the barbecue party,
Ella was
Quite all right!

Good as gold and nice as pie,
She sweetly kissed each guest goodbye
And they all said, "Ella, it's been a pleasure!
Ella, *aren't* you a little treasure!
We're just so sorry we have to go!"

But
little
did
they
know...

7

They didn't know at all
That at the midnight stroke
Ella stirred in her bed
And a *changed* Ella woke

With a furry kind of growl
And hide of yellow and black
And whiskers and golden eyes
And a TAIL at the end of her back!

Softly she loped down the midnight stairs,
In the breathing dark her eyes shone bright,
And she poured herself from the open window
Onto the lawn in the mad moonlight.

TIGERELLA she was!
TIGERELLA her name!
A giant cat of the jungle
By moonlight she became!

Rippling over the silver grass
(She left no mark, she made no sound),
On she moved with flowing shoulders,
Wild One on the midnight ground.

Easily as her shadow
She glided over the wall.
She raised her head in the cornfield,
Seeing, scenting all...

And then she was gathering pace through the whispering barley,
Running, racing, the beat of her heart in tune
With the earth and the night and the creatures~until she coiled
And LEAPT and bit a piece from the rolling moon!

She cuffed the stars about!
Tigerella at play!

How she biffed them,
How she battered them,

How she skittered them,
How she scattered them

Up and down
The Milky Way!

17

And soon through the bright star-clusters
She was travelling on;
By glittering constellations,
She sailed
        at the side
              of the Swan ...

18

Over the great calm lake of space ...

Until she soared and, face to face
And paw to paw, she found the Bear
And they jumbled and tumbled everywhere,
They tussled and hustled, wrestled and nestled,
Two beasts playing together there!

But Mighty Orion the Hunter
Gazed at the stars below.

Mighty Orion the Hunter
Raised his shimmering bow.

He sent an arrow whizzing
Down like a silver streak

Through the billion bits of the heavens
And grazed Tigerella's cheek!

So Tigerella turned
And raced in its track.

She caught it and she wheeled
And hurled that arrow back!

And then they were diving down through the huge unknown.
Wild star-cities they touched and they tumbled beyond,
As they fell through the brain of the night until they landed
On tingling paws
By Ella's
Garden
Pond!

They lapped the water. They licked each other's faces.
"See you again," they said. "So long. Take care."

Then Tigerella poured herself through the window,
And up to his home in the heavens soared the Bear ...

Ella was nice and polite at breakfast,
Ella sat primly
At her place.

Her mother said, "Ella,
Did you sleep all right, dear?
What's that scratch there
On your face?"

Ella said, "Naughty old Tom-cat did it!"
"Did he? The wicked old
So-and-so!"

"Yes," said Ella, "Yes, he did!"

And
little
did
they
know!